On Angel Wings

Michael Morpurgo

illustrated by Quentin Blake

CANDLEWICK PRESS
CAMBRIDGE, MASSACHUSETTS

First U.S. edition 2007

Library of Congress Cataloging-in-Publication Data is available.
Library of Congress Catalog Card Number pending
ISBN 978-0-7636-3466-7

2 4 6 8 10 9 7 5 3 1

Printed in Singapore

This book was typeset in Goudy Old Style.
The illustrations were done in watercolor and ink.

Candlewick Press
2067 Massachusetts Avenue
Cambridge, Massachusetts 02140

visit us at www.candlewick.com

For all the children who read this
on Christmas night
M. M.

*T*he truth is that once we weren't children anymore, we never did believe Grandpa's story, not really—as much as we might have wanted to. It was just too improbable, too fantastical. We still loved listening to it, though. Christmas nights would never have been the same without it.

We'd be out there on the hillside, all of us together, keeping watch over the sheep by night. That's where he'd been on the first Christmas Eve, all those years before, the night it happened— or that's what he told us. We'd be wrapped in *our cloaks and huddled around the fire, the sheep shifting around us in the darkness, and we'd be ready and waiting for the story to begin. That's just how it was last night. Grandpa poked his shepherd's crook into the fire and sent a shower of sparks flying up into the night sky.*

When I was very little, *he began,* I remember I used to think that all the stars were made out of sparks like those, sparks that went on forever, that never went out. Then one night—I'd have been nine, or maybe ten years old—something quite wonderful happened. Father and Uncle Zac were there, and my older brothers, Reuben and Jacob. We were all tired and irritable. It had been a long, hard day. We'd lost a couple of lambs the night before, to a wolf maybe, or a jackal. So no one was singing around the fire that night. No one was even talking. I remember I was stabbing at the fire with my crook, making stars out of the sparks, as I loved to do. Then it happened.

Instead of flying up high to join the stars, the sparks seemed to be playing with one another, then arranging themselves into a figure, a human figure, that was bathed in sudden glorious light,

is believing, isn't it? How would you like to go there? Would you like to see him for yourselves?"

"We'll go; of course we will," said Uncle Zac, getting to his feet. "But you'll have to tell us where to find him. There are dozens of stables in Bethlehem. How are we to know which one he is in?"

"It's simple," the angel Gabriel said. "When I've gone, you'll see a star in the eastern sky. Follow it and it will stop right over the stable. That's where you'll find the baby. What are you waiting for? Do you want to go, or don't you?"

"Why us?" asked Uncle Zac. "Why have you chosen us?"

"No dream," the angel Gabriel replied. "What I am is real, and what I've come to tell you is true. I bring you news of great joy. For tonight, only a few miles away from here, in Bethlehem, a child has been born, a Savior who is Christ the Lord. He will bring peace and goodwill to the whole world. Even as I speak, this child King, this son of God and son of man, is lying wrapped in swaddling clothes and cradled in a manger. I can see from your faces that you don't quite believe me."

"Kings are born in palaces," said Father.

"Not this King," replied the angel. "But seeing

There was a comforting warmth to his voice and a gentleness about him that was instantly reassuring. Uncle Zac and Reuben and Jacob were up on their knees by now, their faces filled not with fear, but with awe and wonder. The sheep were drifting back toward us, gazing up at the angel adoringly as if he were their shepherd. It was Uncle Zac who dared to speak first.

"Are you really an angel?" he breathed.

"I am," said the angel. "My name is Gabriel."

"Are you really real?" Father asked, clutching me as tightly as I was clutching him. "Or are you a dream?"

hovering over us, wings outstretched. It was an angel!

I threw myself into Father's arms and buried my face in his shoulder. When I dared look up again, Uncle Zac and Reuben and Jacob were lying facedown on the ground, Jacob sobbing like a baby. The sheep had scattered everywhere, bleating piteously.

"I'm sorry to drop in on you unexpectedly like this," said the angel. And at the sound of his voice, the sheep fell silent around us. "It must be an awful shock. But believe me, you've got nothing to worry about, nothing at all."

"Because," replied the angel Gabriel, "one day he too will be a shepherd as you are, a shepherd not of sheep, but of all mankind."

"I don't like it," Reuben whispered to Uncle Zac. "How do we know it's true? It could be some sort of a trick to get us to leave our sheep."

"Oh, dear," sighed the angel Gabriel. "I can see you're going to need some convincing."

As he spoke, the sky above was suddenly filled with angels, hundreds of them, and the whole earth rang with their singing:

"Glory to God on high! And on earth, peace, goodwill toward men."

Even as they sang, they hovered above us,
their wings beating the air, so that there was a
great rushing wind all about us that fanned the
embers of the fire into sudden roaring flames.

Reuben and Jacob and Uncle Zac were flat on
their faces again, but I watched. I watched all
the time. I didn't want to miss a thing. I wasn't
frightened at all; I was simply spellbound.

The angels were gone as unexpectedly as they had appeared, and the angel Gabriel too, leaving us alone with our sheep in the silence and the darkness of the hillside. It took a while for our eyes to become accustomed to the dark again. Father threw some more wood onto the fire, and when the sparks flew up I half expected them to become the angel Gabriel again, but this time they just vanished into the blackness above.

"Look," Uncle Zac whispered. "Look up there in the east. That star! It's moving!"

And sure enough, there it was: a moving star low in the eastern sky, as bright a star as I'd ever seen.

"Come on. Let's follow it," Uncle Zac said. "We have to find out if this savior has really come. We have to know if the child King is there."

"What about the sheep?" Father asked. "Who'll look after the sheep? We can't just leave them."

"Well, I'm not staying," said Reuben and Jacob in unison.

And suddenly everyone was looking at me, and I could see at once the way it was going.

"Why me?" I protested. "What about the wolves? What about the jackals?"

"He's frightened of the dark," Jacob scoffed. "He's a scaredy cat."

"You've got the fire," Uncle Zac told me. "They won't come near the fire."

"We won't be gone long, son." Father might have sounded more sympathetic than my brothers, but he was still going with them. They were still leaving me alone. "Bethlehem's just over the hill. We'll be back before dawn."

"But we could take the sheep with us," I pleaded. "Then we could all go."

"You can't move sheep in the dark, stupid," Reuben said.

"But why me?" I cried. "It's just because I'm the youngest. It's not fair." No one was listening.

"Don't worry," said Father, trying to console me as they made ready to go. "We'll tell you all about the baby when we get back. Promise. You just keep the fire going and look after the sheep. You'll be quite safe."

And off they went, shadows drifting away into the night, leaving me. I had never felt so alone, nor so miserable as I did then. Sitting by the fire, pulling my cloak around me, I cursed my luck for being the youngest and my father for abandoning me, and began to cry.

Lifting my head, I let out a huge wail

of anger and despair that echoed over the hills: "It's not fair! It's not fair!"

As the echoes died, I became suddenly aware that I was not alone anymore. There, opposite me in the glowing light of the fire, sat the angel Gabriel.

"You don't sound very happy," he said. "They left you behind, didn't they? Well, someone had to look after the sheep, I suppose."

"I suppose," I said, so relieved not to be alone anymore.

"You're right, though," said the angel Gabriel, "about life not being fair. So I've had this idea to make it a little fairer. I could fly you to the stable. We could be there and back, lickety-split, and no one would ever know you'd been gone."

"You could fly me there?" I cried, more excited than I had been in all my life. "You could really do that?"

"Easy as pie," he said.

At that moment, a sheep and her lamb came and lay down beside me, as if to remind me of my duty. I knew I couldn't leave them.

"The sheep," I said, suddenly downcast. "There'd be no one to look after the sheep."

"Have you forgotten my heavenly chorus?" said the angel Gabriel. "They don't just sing, you know."

And even as he spoke, the sky above us burst into light, and out of the light they came floating down—who knows how many?—landing softly on their feet among the sheep, who seemed not in the least alarmed.

"Enough to do the job, I think, don't you?" said the angel Gabriel with a laugh. "Now, hop on. We haven't a moment to lose."

I did as he told me. Still clutching my shepherd's crook, I vaulted onto his back and held on. So I left the sheep with their guardian angels and lifted off, my arms around the angel Gabriel's neck.

"Hang on," he said, laughing, "but don't strangle me—there's a good boy."

And so we rose into the sky, leaving the sheep below with the guardian angels now as their shepherds.

On we flew along black glassy rivers, up and down hills, his great wings beating strongly, slowly. And always we went eastward, the star ahead of us, beckoning us on. I wanted it to go on forever and ever, even though the cold numbed my fingers, numbed my face, and made my eyes water.

I saw the lights of the little town flickering beneath us. We saw where the star had stopped, saw the lights of the stable below. We floated gently to earth in the courtyard of an inn.

The town lay asleep all around us, still and silent, except for a couple of dogs that barked at each other. Cats slunk everywhere into dark alleyways, their eyes glinting.

"You go in alone," said the angel Gabriel. "His mother is called Mary; his father is Joseph. Off you go now."

The guttering glow of yellow lamplight seemed to be inviting me in. The door was half open. I stepped through.

It was much like any other stable I'd been in—warm and dusty and smelly. A couple of donkeys were lying side by side, their great ears following me, their eyes watching me with dreamy indifference. In the dim light of the stable I could see several oxen chewing their cud, grunting contentedly.

One of them licked deep into her nose as I passed by. I could still see no baby, no Christ child, no King. I was beginning to wonder if the angel had brought me to the wrong place. Then from a stall at the far end of the stable came a man's voice.

"We're over here," he said. "Where the sheep are. Careful you don't tread on them."

The sheep shifted as I walked slowly among them. A lamb came skittering out of the shadows and suckled his mother furiously, his tail waggling with wild delight.

It was then I saw them, at last, their faces bright in the lamplight.

"Come closer," said Mary. "You won't be disturbing him. He's wide awake."

She was sitting propped up in the hay, the baby cradled in her arms. All I could see of him was a pink face and one tiny hand, which he waved a little and then promptly shoved into his mouth. He was looking at me, straight at me, and when at last he took his fist out of his mouth, he smiled, and it was a smile I have never forgotten, a smile of such love that it moves my heart to this day whenever I think of it.

I crouched down in the straw beside them, and when I offered him my finger, he clung to it and didn't seem to want to let go.

"He's strong," I said.

"He'll need to be," said Joseph.

We talked in whispers, the three of us, and Joseph told me how ashamed he was not to have found a better place for Mary to give birth, but that everywhere in Bethlehem, all the inns were full.

"It's fine," said Mary. "It's warm in here, and this manger's full of soft hay for a cradle. He has all he needs, and now he has his first visitor. Would you like to hold him for a while?"

I had never in all my life held a baby before—
plenty of lambs, but never a baby. Joseph showed
me how to do it. Babies were easier, I discovered.
They didn't wriggle so much.

"What's he called?" I asked, cradling him in my arms, hoping against hope that he wouldn't cry.

"Jesus," Mary said. "We're calling him Jesus."

So for a few precious minutes I held him in my arms, the child that has been the light of my life ever since.

I stayed until they laid him in his manger of hay, until he fell asleep, and Mary too. Then Joseph took me back through the sheep to the stable door to say good-bye.

"There may be more visitors tonight," said Joseph. "But you were the first. We shan't forget you."

"Nor I you," I replied. It was only then, as I was about to go, that it occurred to me I had forgotten something.

"Whenever a child is born in our village," I said, "everyone brings a gift. This is all I've got with me." And I handed Joseph my shepherd's crook. "Father made it for me. He said it should last a lifetime."

"Thank you," Joseph said, running his hand along the crook. "This is wonderful work, the work of a craftsman. He will have no finer gift than this." And with that he turned and went back inside.

Moments later the angel Gabriel was winging
me away, out over the walls of the stable
yard, over the sleeping town, away
from the light of the star, and
back toward the darkness
of the hills.

As we flew, I was full of questions. I wanted to know so much about Jesus, this child King who was going to save the world.

"How will he do it?" I shouted into Gabriel's ear against the sound of the wind. "How will he bring us peace and goodwill?"

The angel Gabriel flew on, never answering any of my questions. It was almost as if he hadn't heard me at all. Only when we landed among the sheep and the shepherd angels did he at last give me an answer.

"Love," he said. "He will bring us love, and through love we will at last have peace and goodwill on earth. Now, make sure you keep the fire going— there's a good boy."

Those were the last words he spoke to me. There were no good-byes. There was no time. He rose at once into the night sky, and with him all the other angels too, each a beacon of sparkling light. And as they went, I heard first the singing of their wings and then the singing of their voices, until the sky above me and the whole earth rang with such a joyful sound that I thought my heart would burst.

"Glory to God on high! And on earth, peace, goodwill toward men."

Slowly the music faded and the light died. I felt suddenly alone in the night, until the sheep gathered

about me, all of us, I know, sharing the wonder of everything we had just witnessed.

Father and the others came back just after sunrise, full of everything, of course, and very pleased with themselves. They'd followed the star and found the stable and the child King wrapped in swaddling clothes. He'd been fast asleep in his manger, they said, all the time they were there.

"Such a pity you couldn't have been with us," Reuben said with a snigger.

"Then these three Kings from far-off Persian lands turned up, and there wasn't room for us

and we had to go," said Uncle Zac, who sounded more than a little put out. "You should've seen the presents they brought: gold, frankincense, myrrh. We had nothing to give him except our crooks, and we could hardly give him those, could we?"

"Proper stupid we felt," Jacob added.

"Sheep all right?" Father asked me. "Anything happen while we were gone?"

"Not a thing," I replied. "Not a thing."

I nearly told them then, so nearly. I was bursting to tell them everything. But I didn't, because I knew they'd never believe me anyway. Reuben and Jacob would only have scoffed and laughed at me even more than usual. "Just keep quiet about it," I told myself. "When the time comes, you can tell your children and your grandchildren, because they'll know about Jesus by then—everyone will." And you do too, don't you, his whole life, everything he did and said? You may not believe my story, but you don't laugh at me; you don't scoff. You just think I'm a bit past it, a bit fanciful in my old age. And I suppose I am at that.

And Grandpa always ended his story the same way, his voice almost a whisper. And that shepherd's crook I gave him—I told Father I'd lost it in the dark that night, and he made me another—Jesus carried it with him all his life. It was there at the Sermon on the Mount, when he fed the five thousand, when he rode into Jerusalem. He had it with him almost to the end, till they took it off him, till that last day when he carried the cross instead.

And so Grandpa finished his
story. But that wasn't the end of
it, not last night. Last night the story
had a very different ending altogether, something
amazing, incredible—which is why I've written
it down. This way, I'll always be able to remember
it as it was and I'll never be able to believe it
didn't happen.

As we sat there around the fire, silent in our
thoughts, I thought, as all of us did, that Grandpa's
Christmas story was over for another year. It was
such a lovely story, but just a story. We knew how
Grandpa had followed Jesus all his life, how much

he loved him. Wishful thinking, we thought, that's all it had been, just wishful thinking. But I remember sitting there last night and wondering whether any of it could possibly be true. That was when it happened.

Grandpa began prodding at the fire with his shepherd's crook. Showers of sparks rose into the night sky, and as I watched them, I saw that they did not fly up toward the stars, but gathered themselves

into a great light. Within the light I saw beacons of brightness that took shape and became angels, hundreds of them, thousands of them, their wings singing in the air, then their voices too, until the skies above us rang with such joyful sounds that I thought my heart would burst.

"Glory to God on high!" they sang. "And on earth, peace, goodwill toward men!"